D0852101

CALGARY PUBLIC LIBRARY

DEC - - 2012

SNOWMAN MAGIC

By Katherine Tegen

Illustrated by Brandon Dorman

HARPER
An Imprint of HarperCollinsPublishers

To my parents
—K.B.T.

With thanks to Maria

For our Kayla-Bird down south,
sending a bit of snow your way
—B.D.

Snowman Magic

Text copyright © 2012 by Katherine Tegen

Illustrations copyright © 2012 by Brandon Dorman

All rights reserved. Manufactured in China.

No part of this book may be used or reproduced in any manner whatsoever without

written permission except in the case of brief quotations embodied in critical articles

and reviews. For information address HarperCollins Children's Books, a division of

HarperCollins Publishers, 10 East 53rd Street, New York, NY 10022.

www.harpercollinschildrens.com

Library of Congress Cataloging-in-Publication Data is available.

ISBN 978-0-06-201445-0 (trade bdg.)

Typography by Rachel Zegar

12 13 14 15 16 SCP 10 9 8 7 6 5 4 3 2 1

❖

First Edition

"Snowmen fall from the sky unassembled."
—Anonymous

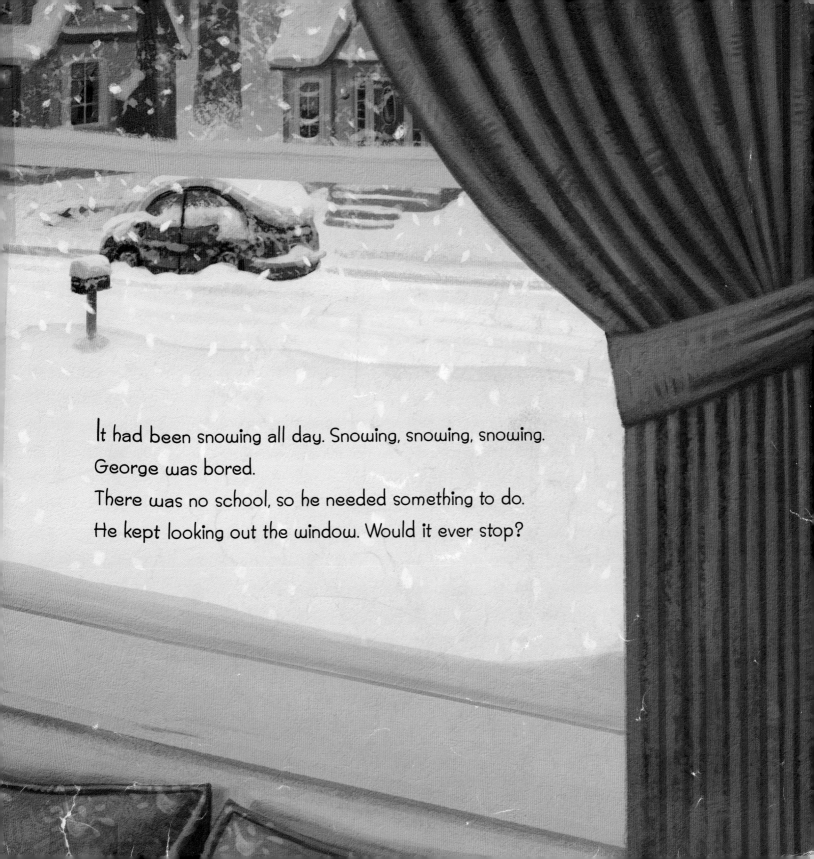

It had been snowing all day. Snowing, snowing, snowing.
George was bored.
There was no school, so he needed something to do.
He kept looking out the window. Would it ever stop?

The next morning, the sun was shining.

When George looked out the window, everything was a brilliant white.

The snow was so bright, it was almost hard to look at.

If he squinted, he could see it was very deep, and it had drifted high against the slope in his backyard.

George put on his warm socks, and
his snow pants, and his flannel shirt.

Then he put on his snow jacket,
his boots, his mittens, and his hat.

He was ready.

Outside, the air smelled clean and cold.

George plunged into the snow. It was fluffy, but crunchy too.

He made a snowball and threw it against a tree.

It was very, very quiet.

George took some snow and packed it into a small ball.

Then he started rolling the ball in the snow. The ball got bigger . . . and bigger.

When the ball got too heavy to roll, he stopped rolling it near the bottom of the slope.

Then he started rolling a
medium-sized ball.

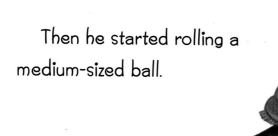

He put it on top of the big ball.

Finally, he made a small
ball for the top.

George went inside the house and found a scarf in the closet and a carrot in the refrigerator.

In the old days, his mother told him, people used to take pieces of coal and use them to make eyes.

But there wasn't any coal in George's house.

So he found two buttons and brought them outside with the scarf and the carrot.

He carefully pushed the buttons
into the small ball near the top.

He stuck the carrot in the center.

He found a few small twigs and used them
to make a mouth.

He wrapped the scarf between the top
ball and the middle ball.

And he found two branches to stick into
the sides of the middle ball.

It was a perfect snowman.

George turned his head. He thought he
saw the snowman smiling at him.
Could it be?

"Time for a snack," said George.

He went inside the house and got two mugs of hot chocolate and some cookies.

He put them on the snow table.

"Would you like something to eat?" George asked.

"I can't drink hot chocolate," the snowman said, "but a cookie would be nice."

It was
MAGIC.

After their snack, George made a cave, tunneling deep into the slope.

He piled up snowballs at the entrance.

Then he threw a couple at the snowman.

The snowman made some snowballs and threw them back at George.

His long branch arms helped him throw the snowballs very far.

It was hard to say who won the fight, but it was still fun.

The snowman chased George around the yard,
and then George chased the snowman.

The snowman couldn't move that fast, so it was
easy for George to sneak up on him.

It was starting to get dark.

George didn't want to go inside, but his mother was calling him.

"Good-bye, Snowman," he said. "I will see you tomorrow."

George thought he heard the snowman say, "Good night."

The next day it was warmer.

The sun was even brighter, and the snowman was shrinking.

George played with him all day, but he could tell that the snowman didn't have quite the same energy.

Then it was Monday.

George had to go to school.

It was another bright, warm day.

When he came home, the snowman was almost gone.

The scarf and the carrot and the buttons had slid down.

He could hardly recognize his snowman.

The cave had collapsed too, and the snow table had melted.

The next morning, George looked out the window.
It was snowing! Snowing, snowing, snowing.
He couldn't wait . . .

to build his snowman again!